FANNY AND SARAH

FANNY AND

A Windswept Book

Windswept House   Washington, D.C.

SARAH

BY JANE D. WEINBERGER

Illustrated by Karen MacDonald

10   9   8   7   6   5

Printed in the United States of America
for the publishers by
Down East Graphics

FANNY AND SARAH

ONCE there were two friends, Sarah and Fanny. Everyone thought how odd it was for them to be such good friends for they were very unalike. Fanny was a black cat and Sarah was a white duck. What seemed odd for others was just natural for them. They had known each other since Fanny was a wee kitten and Sarah a fuzzy little duckling. They both lived on a farm in the country with Mary Jane and her mother and father.

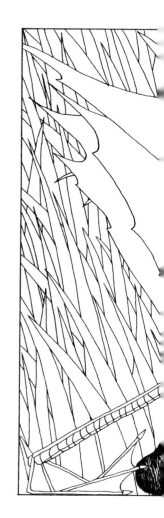

Sarah had a nest of eggs under the willow tree. While she sat on them to keep them warm, Fanny sat beside her to keep her company on the long summer afternoons. The two friends were blissfully unaware of the people who came to look at them saying "How unusual" and "Aren't they funny" and other silly things as if friends had to be just alike.

Fanny had many jobs to do about the farm. She
had to scare the mice from the barn, chase the

chipmunks from the garden and frighten the birds
who tried to eat the seeds as fast as they were planted.

But she left all of these duties to sit on the nest while Sarah went to swim in the pond.

Fanny was a faithful friend and she went every afternoon to keep the eggs warm while Sarah had her bath.

Even Mary Jane laughed to see a cat sitting on a duck's nest. Fanny did not care. Sarah was her friend and needed her help. Inside the eggs baby ducks were growing and they had to be kept warm until they were big enough to peck their way out of the shells.

One day while Sarah was bathing and Fanny was sitting on the eggs, a terrible thing happened. A naughty bad boy caught Sarah and put her in a big plastic bag. He carried her home to his yard and put her in a pen from which she could not escape.

Fanny waited and waited for Sarah to return. She was growing hungry. It was supper time and she could hear Mary Jane calling her, "Here, Fanny, Fanny— where are you?" But she could not leave the eggs. Soon Mary Jane stopped calling. It grew dark and very cold, still Sarah did not come.

Fanny stayed there all the long night waiting and worrying. She was stiff and cold, still she kept Sarah's eggs warm. The next day Mary Jane found her. "So that's where you are. Come in the house, you silly cat, it is going to rain. Where is Sarah? That duck should be sitting on her own nest," Mary Jane scolded.

Fanny wanted to go with Mary Jane. She wished she could go into the nice warm house. But, she knew she had to keep the eggs warm until Sarah came back. So she stayed on the nest.

Meanwhile, at the home of that thoughtless boy, Sarah was working to escape. She was digging a hole under the fence—scratching and scratching—it was hard work and she had to stop to rest now and then. She knew it was almost time for her baby ducklings to come out of the eggs and she was very worried. The thought of her babies made her scratch harder and harder.

Fanny stretched a bit and shook herself in an effort to keep warm. Then she heard a cracking sound and a chirping noise. She moved off the nest shaking the water off her back. She watched in amazement as each egg cracked open, one, two, three, four, five, and out of each a damp, yellow chick appeared.

Sarah's babies, five tiny ducklings. They soon found their legs and began to move about. Fanny was puzzled as to what she should do with them. They were not much like kittens.

She knew she should get them to some place safe, so she led them to Mary Jane. It was a strange sight, a black cat with five ducklings following her. She was very proud to bring them to Mary Jane who knew just what to do. She put them into a tub full of water where they began to swim at once.

Just then with a great flapping and squawking Sarah flew into the yard. She had finally dug a deep enough hole under the fence and escaped.

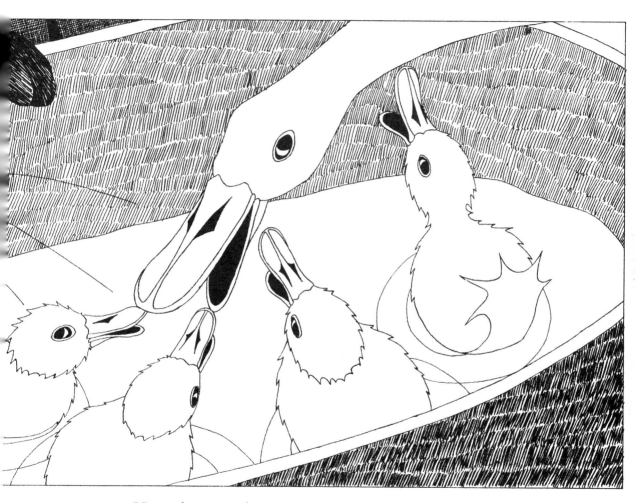

How happy she was to see her ducklings
swimming in the tub. Fanny had saved her babies.

A friend in need is a friend indeed.